Investigator™

in

CLASSROOM CAPERS

by Jerry Smath

Troll Associates

Dear Reader,
  You can be an investigator, too! Just figure out the puzzles that appear throughout the story, and help Investigator solve these *Classroom Capers.*

To Matthew Kleckner
—J.S.

One morning Investigator's niece Gabby and her parents stopped by Investigator's house before school.

"Can you help us?" asked Gabby's mother. "Today is Parents' Day at Gabby's school and we were both called in to work. Could you go with her in our place?"

★ How can you tell that Investigator was asleep?
★ Gabby's parents are dressed for work. What are their jobs?
★ Are their hats and coats the same?

"Of course I'll go with Gabby!" said the great detective. "But what do I have to do?"

"It's very simple," said Gabby's father. "Just tell the children in her class all about your job."

Investigator changed his clothes and packed his bag right away. Gabby's folks gave her a big hug before they went off to work.

"Why don't you play with my pet mouse while you're waiting?" said Investigator.

Gabby looked all over for the little mouse, but she could not find him.

★ Where is the mouse hiding?
★ Is the cocoa in the cup hot or cold?
★ What is missing from the kitchen door? Can you find it?
★ Find five butterflies in this picture.

When Investigator and Gabby arrived at school the kids and some of their parents were already there.

"This is going to be so much fun!" said Gabby.

Just then she saw her best friend, Penny, and waved.

★ Which kid is Gabby's best friend?

★ Mrs. Bear is walking her pets. How many pets got loose? Where are they?

Ms. Ostrich was Gabby's teacher. She greeted Investigator and the parents as they came into the classroom.

"I have made each of you a name card," said Ms. Ostrich. "The name cards will tell the children who you are."

When the class saw the name cards, they all giggled. Investigator knew why!

★ Can you match the right name card to each person?
★ Which math answer is wrong?

"Mrs. Rabbit is a farmer," said the teacher, "and she has brought something interesting to show you."

"Here are my fast-growing Silly Seeds!" said Mrs. Rabbit. She gave each child some water and a cup of dirt to plant the seeds.

Investigator watched the kids at work. "Some of you are not planting your seeds correctly," he said.

★ How many kids are planting their seeds wrong?
What are they doing wrong?

Once all the seeds were planted correctly, the kids
stood back and watched them grow.

ZOOM . . . Each plant shot high up into the air. But
they were not all the same. Farmer Rabbit's Silly Seeds
grew to be very silly plants.

Investigator examined each plant carefully. "Hmmmm,
very interesting," said the supersleuth.

★ How many plants have fruit?
★ How many plants have vegetables?
★ How many have both?
★ How many have none?

Next, Mr. Cat, the baker, pushed a big oven into the classroom.

"Today I am going to bake cupcakes!" he said. "But I will need your help."

Everyone mixed flour, eggs, butter, and honey in a big bowl.

★ How many eggs were used?
★ Who has lost a spoon? Can you find it?

Then Mr. Cat poured the batter into a cupcake tin and put it into the oven. But something went wrong. They waited and waited, but the cupcakes never baked. "I know what's wrong!" said Investigator.

★ Why didn't the cupcakes bake?

Mr. Cat baked six cupcakes—one cupcake for each student, and a special chocolate one for Ms. Ostrich.

But when he turned around to shut the oven door, two of the cupcakes were gone.

"They have already been eaten!" cried Investigator. "And I know who did it!"

★ Who ate the cupcakes?
★ Who ate the teacher's cupcake by mistake?
★ Who doesn't like cupcakes at all?

"Now it's my turn!" said Mrs. Pig, the pilot.
She took out five paper airplanes and gave them
to the children.
"We will have a contest," said Mrs. Pig. "Whoever flies
his or her plane the highest will win this pair of wings."

"They're pretty," said Penny, "but they all look the same."
"Look again!" said Investigator with a smile.

★ Which plane is a different color?
★ Which plane has a different tail?
★ Which plane has two sets of wings?
★ Which plane has a different nose?

Mrs. Pig gave the signal. "Ready, get set, throw!"
The paper airplanes flew all around the classroom.
"I don't see my airplane anywhere!" said Gabby.
"I do," said her uncle. "And I also know who won
the prize."

★ Whose plane did the most loops?
★ Whose plane did not fly far at all?
★ Who won the prize?

The next parent to talk to the class was Mr. Fox, the carpenter.

He brought in some wood and piled it on the floor.

"I will build a birdhouse," he said. "But first I must find my tools."

★ How many hidden tools can you find?

After Mr. Fox found his tools, he sawed and hammered.
When he was finished he had built a beautiful birdhouse.
   Investigator looked at the birdhouse,
then handed the carpenter a drill.
   "I'm afraid it's not finished yet!" he said.

★ What is missing on the birdhouse?

"Let's put up the birdhouse now!" said Ms. Ostrich.
Everyone followed her outside to the school yard.

Mr. Fox quickly climbed up the tree and hung the
birdhouse. But when it was time to come down he was
afraid. "Help me!" he cried.

Investigator reached into his bag and pulled out a ladder . . . but it was too short.

★ What else came out of the bag?
★ Seven birds want to use the birdhouse. Can you find them?
★ How many birds will not fit through the hole?

"EEEK!" screamed Ms. Ostrich
when she saw Investigator's mouse.

★ Find four things that Ms. Ostrich has lost.

She jumped so high that she landed in the tree next to Mr. Fox.

"Help!" cried Ms. Ostrich. "I'm afraid to come down, too!"

Investigator knew just what to do! He reached into his bag again and took out a phone. "I'll call the fire station!" he said.

★ The mouse is hiding again. Can you find him?

Within minutes a bright red truck came driving down the street. It screeched to a stop at the school.

★ Who did not see the truck go by?
★ Why couldn't they see it?
★ Which house looks empty?

"It's Mommy and Daddy!" called Gabby.
Quickly, Gabby's parents put a long ladder
up to the tree. Then, as everyone cheered, they
carried Ms. Ostrich and Mr. Fox to safety.
"It looks like your folks came to Parents' Day
after all," said Investigator, chuckling.

★ Some of the parents have lost their hats. Who gets which hat?
★ Who has found the teacher's shoe?
★ Who has found her book?

"Now we know what your parents do for a living," said Gabby's teacher, "but what does your uncle do?"

"Why, can't you see?" said Gabby proudly. "He solves mysteries! There's no detective greater than my uncle Investigator!"

★ There are two new kids in this picture. Do you see them?